POPULAR CULTURE

A VIEW FROM THE PAPARAZZI

Orlando Bloom

John Legend

Kelly Clarkson

Lindsay Lohan

Johnny Depp

Mandy Moore

Hilary Duff

Ashlee and
Jessica Simpson

Will Ferrell

Justin
Timberlake

Jake Gyllenhaal

Paris and
Nicky Hilton

Owen and
Luke Wilson

LeBron James

Tiger Woods

Lindsay Lohan

Hal Marcovitz

Mason Crest Publishers

Lindsay Lohan

FRONTIS
The talented actress and singer Lindsay Lohan has emerged as one of today's most popular young entertainers.

Produced by 21st Century Publishing and Communications, Inc.

MASON CREST PUBLISHERS INC.
370 Reed Road
Broomall, Pennsylvania 19008
(866) MCP-BOOK (toll free)
www.masoncrest.com

Printed in the United States.

First Printing

9 8 7 6 5 4 3 2 1

Library of Congress Cataloging-in-Publication Data

Marcovitz, Hal.
   Lindsay Lohan / Hal Marcovitz.
     p. cm. — (Pop culture: a view from the paparazzi)
   Includes bibliographical references and index.
   Hardback edition: ISBN-13: 978-1-4222-0206-7
   Paperback edition: ISBN-13: 978-1-4222-0361-3
  1. Lohan, Lindsay, 1986–   —Juvenile literature. 2. Actors—United States—Biography—Juvenile literature. I. Title.
PN2287.L623M37 2007
791.4302'8092—dc22
[B]   2007008988

Publisher's notes:
- All quotations in this book come from original sources, and contain the spelling and grammatical inconsistencies of the original text.

- The Web sites mentioned in this book were active at the time of publication. The publisher is not responsible for Web sites that have changed their addresses or discontinued operation since the date of publication. The publisher will review and update the Web site addresses each time the book is reprinted.

CONTENTS

Lindsay's breakout role came in the hit 2004 film *Mean Girls*, which was loosely based on a nonfiction book about the pressures that young girls face in school. In the film Lindsay's character, Cady Heron, must deal with bullying, gossiping, and backstabbing among the popular girls at her new school.

1

Taking on the Mean Girls

Few films released in 2004 struck a chord with teenage girls as much as *Mean Girls*. Many girls could identify with the plight of the main character, Cady Heron, in her cursed relations with the high school's popular crowd. This bond viewers felt was largely the result of the convincing performance of the actress playing Cady, teenage sensation Lindsay Lohan.

Fans of the movie also recognized something familiar in the girls who plague Cady. They are known as "the Plastics"—the really cool girls who wear the most stylish clothes and jewelry, go to the best parties, and date the best-looking boys. When 16-year-old Cady first walks into North Shore High School, after living her life until that point in the densest of African jungles, she is innocent to the threat posed by the Plastics, who consist of Gretchen, Karen, and the group's "Queen Bee," Regina George.

Home-schooled by her **zoologist** parents, Cady wasn't prepared for the Plastics' lying, cheating, backstabbing, and other truly mean behavior. But as she soon learns, this high school's jungle is not that much different from the real jungle where she had grown up.

Mean Girls emerged as one of the hit movies of 2004. Actress and singer Lindsay Lohan was just 18 years old when the film was released, and so she had very clear memories of life as a high school student. She told an interviewer for *Life Story* magazine,

> **"In school, there are a lot of bullies and stuff like that, or girls who think that they're better than other people, and it's just a waste of time. It's so unattractive when someone is going to go and talk down to someone else for no reason unless someone really does something to hurt you and it's intentional."**

Natural Talent

Although just a teenager when *Mean Girls* came out, Lindsay was already a veteran actress at this stage. She had done six previous movies, including *The Parent Trap*, a family film released when she was just eight years old. Thus, it became common for her to receive scripts from **producers** who wanted her to appear in their films. While most actors often find it is difficult to settle on a particular project, doing *Mean Girls* was a no-brainer for Lindsay. In the *Life Story* interview, she explained how she was sold on making the movie and playing the role of Cady. She said,

> **"I was kind of obsessed with [the script]. It's smart and it's edgy and it's quick and witty. It's something that girls can relate to in high school. It's not something that girls my age will go and see and be like, 'Okay, that never happened in my school.' It has every little detail down to like the three-way calling and stuff. I think that's really cool to watch on screen."**

Mean Girls was written by *Saturday Night Live* cast member Tina Fey, who also played the role of a math teacher in the movie. With

Mean Girls, Fey was focused on making the transition from acting on television to acting in a movie. Although she is several years older than Lindsay, during filming Fey took many cues from the teenage actress. "I would watch Lindsay to learn what it is to be a film actor," Fey told *People* magazine.

Fey could tell that Lindsay was a natural for the part and would have little trouble filling the role of Cady. Lindsay was, after all, a teenage girl herself. Like Cady, she spent hours glued to her cell phone,

Lindsay described her own school experiences to interviewer Lynda Obst: "I was more of a floater in high school. I made it a point to get along with everyone because if you're an actress, people assume that you think you're better than everyone else. I wanted to make sure that people had no reason to think that about me."

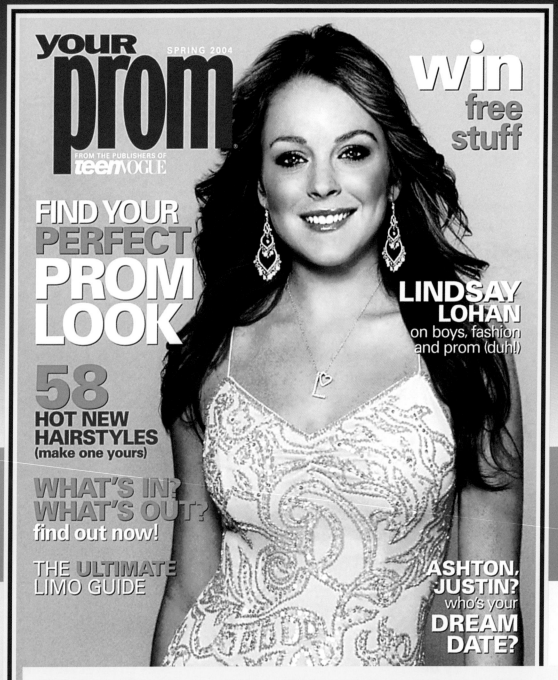

your prom SPRING 2004

FROM THE PUBLISHERS OF
teenVOGUE

win free stuff

FIND YOUR **PERFECT PROM LOOK**

58 HOT NEW HAIRSTYLES (make one yours)

WHAT'S IN? WHAT'S OUT? find out now!

THE ULTIMATE LIMO GUIDE

LINDSAY LOHAN on boys, fashion and prom (duh!)

ASHTON, JUSTIN? who's your **DREAM DATE?**

Thanks to the success of *Mean Girls*, which earned more than $200 million at the box office, Lindsay became highly sought after as a model, as well as for leading roles in other films. She began appearing on many magazine covers, including this issue of the teen magazine *Your Prom* in 2004.

or constantly surfed the Internet looking for the hottest clothes or shoes. Said Fey,

> **"[She] was really a teenager. She'd be on her pink cell phone calling her mom or online trying to track down baby-blue Uggs."**

Turning Point

Mean Girls proved to be a tremendous success by earning more than $200 million at the box office at theaters in the United States and other countries. It also received widespread praise from critics, who at first prepared themselves for another run-of-the-mill teen comedy. They were surprised that *Mean Girls* could capture so accurately the humor, fear, and sadness that marked the life of a teenage girl in America. Writing in the entertainment newspaper *Variety*, film critic David Rooney said,

> **"[T]his sassy if wildly uneven comedy navigates the treacherous high school jungle that separates cool cliques from wannabes, wading through some nasty behavior before delivering its moral message. . . . Lohan displays plenty of charm, verve and deft comic timing as she switches between innocence and craftiness. The actress has a confidence, strength of character and unforced feistiness that make her an empowering mascot for young girls."**

While Lindsay was already a star when the film was released, *Mean Girls* would mark a turning point in her career. Before, she was known mostly for light comedies and family entertainment, such as the Walt Disney studio productions of *The Parent Trap* and *Freaky Friday*. Her performance in *Mean Girls* proved she was ready for much meatier roles.

In addition to doing more serious work in film, she was now able to branch out and follow her ambition to be a recording artist. In 2004 she released her debut album, *Speak*, which went on to sell over a million copies. However, pursuing more opportunities also meant living a more complicated life. Adulthood and a life in front of the camera lens brought their share of trials for this budding star.

Lindsay appears in an advertising photograph, 2004. She started her career as a model when she was only three years old, appearing in dozens of television commercials (including a Jell-O pudding ad with comedian Bill Cosby and print advertisements, many for the company Toys "R" Us) by the time she was a teenager.

2

Headed for Stardom

Even at the age of three, it was clear that red-headed, freckled Lindsay Lohan was born to be a star. That's when she started working as a model, appearing in print advertisements and TV commercials. Among her early **gigs** was a Jell-O commercial with comedian Bill Cosby. She also appeared in commercials for Pizza Hut, Wendy's, and the Gap.

Although TV commercials are typically not considered demanding work for actors, they still can pose challenges. Actors have to learn lines, play their roles convincingly, and display their talents—all tough requirements for a child actor. But Lindsay, who eventually appeared in some 60 different TV commercials, was up for the job. She told *Life Story*,

> **"I have a photographic memory, and I was always able to remember my lines, which made me a favorite for commercials. It's always helpful when the people hiring you don't have to worry about you—you get a reputation as someone who can do the job, and then everyone wants to hire you."**

Suburban Lifestyle

Lindsay may have attained stardom early on, but her home was not always in Hollywood. Born Lindsay Dee Lohan on July 2, 1986, she grew up in comfortable suburban homes in Cold Spring Harbor and Merrick, both on Long Island, located east of New York City. She is the oldest of four children. Her two younger brothers, Dakota and Michael, and a younger sister, Aliana, are all aspiring actors or models.

That all of Lindsay's siblings have their sights on Hollywood should not come as a surprise, because their mother, Dina Lohan, also has a background in the performing arts. A former professional dancer on Broadway, Dina had appeared in the shows *Cats* and *A Chorus Line*. She also performed in Radio City Music Hall as one of its Rockettes, the high-stepping dancers who perform their famous routines during major holidays and throughout the year.

With the exception of her acting and modeling careers, Lindsay had a pretty normal upbringing. She was baptized in a Catholic church and attended public schools throughout her childhood. At home, however, things were not always rosy. Her father, Michael Lohan, argued often with Dina. Their fights usually ended by him leaving the house. Lindsay told *Vanity Fair* magazine,

> **"It got to the point where my father would not come home for a few days. He would come home . . . and be very angry, and we'd be walking on eggshells, and it would be a very tense, scary household."**

Her father, a businessman, was also a drug abuser and would later serve prison sentences for **fraud** and other offenses. Having spent many years of Lindsay's life in jail, Michael barely knew his daughter.

Lindsay arrives at the premiere of her 2006 film *A Prairie Home Companion* with her mother, Dina (right), and younger sister Ali (left). Dina had been a professional dancer in New York City before marrying Michael Lohan, Lindsay's father, and she encouraged Lindsay to pursue a career in show business.

Several times during Michael's time away from jail, Dina, fearing that her husband was a threat to the family's safety, moved out with the children. Eventually, a court ordered Michael to stay away from his wife and children.

Limitless Talent

While her father's legal problems may have thrown Lindsay's personal life into turmoil, her professional career as an actress seemed limitless. After making her mark in TV commercials, as well as in a comic sketch on the comedy/talk show *Late Night with David Letterman*, Lindsay landed her first steady job as a dramatic actress at the age of 10 when she was signed for the role of Ali Fowler on the daytime drama *Another World*.

Acting in daytime dramas, also known as soap operas, can be grueling work because a new episode is filmed each day. Actors must learn their lines quickly and, with little time to practice, give convincing performances. Lindsay rose to the occasion, balancing a busy schedule between school and the studio. Since at the time Lindsay was still attending public school, she would go to classes four days a week then spend the other day at the *Another World* studio in New York.

All her scenes were filmed in one long, tedious day. Although the stint as Ali lasted only seven months, Lindsay and the show's crew shot enough scenes with her character to fill two years of episodes. In her *Life Story* interview, Lindsay recalled,

> **"Each experience is great on its own. I love acting and it's something I want to do forever, so I'm grateful for all the opportunities I had. Working on a soap, where you have to learn pages and pages of lines, gave me great practice for the future."**

The Parent Trap

Lindsay needed practice to meet the acting challenges of her first feature-length movie, *The Parent Trap*, in 1998. She took on not one but two different roles, playing characters from different countries and with different accents. The Disney movie was going to be a remake of the 1961 hit starring Hayley Mills. Like the original *Parent Trap*, whose main characters were twin girls separated at birth, the remake

In the 1998 Disney film *The Parent Trap*, Lindsay played the two main characters: Annie James (left) and Hallie Parker, two identical twins who did not know the other existed until an unexpected meeting at a summer camp. The girls become friends and eventually conspire to bring their parents back together.

would only use one actress to play both roles (although the characters were renamed).

Before settling on Lindsay, the film's producers launched a national search to find a star for the film. After scouring the country they identified five young actresses who they believed could pull off the double role. Lindsay and four other actresses were called in for auditions, which were staged in a Hollywood studio. One of the film's producers, Charles Shyer, recalled,

> **"Lindsay was the first one up. I leaned over to [director] Nancy [Meyers] and said, 'This one is going to be hard to beat. She's just a winner.' The minute the cameras rolled, something happened with Lindsay. It was just that magical 'it' you can't describe."**

Two Roles

Filming *The Parent Trap* would prove to be a much different experience for Lindsay than her previous acting work. For starters, because the movie would be shot on location—some scenes in London, and others in the northern California region known as the Napa Valley—Lindsay was required to spend months away from home. Because she could not attend regular school, she set aside time to work with a personal **tutor**.

But the biggest difference between *The Parent Trap* and Lindsay's other work as an actress was that in this case she was the star. In all her commercials, her work on camera never spanned for more than a minute. And in *Another World*, she was simply one member of a very large cast. But now, Lindsay would appear on screen for virtually the entire two-hour movie. Adding to the challenge, she had to play two separate roles, which meant developing separate accents and mannerisms for the character of Hallie, who was from California, and for her twin sister Annie, from London.

The original film had relied on stand-ins to provide the illusion that Sharon and Susan were separate individuals. For instance, when Sharon spoke to Susan, the camera would usually focus on Sharon while an anonymous actress, shot from behind, acted as Susan's stand-in, with only the back of her head in view. In order to give the newer version a more realistic feel, the movie's producers decided to show the faces of both twins on the screen at the same time. And so, for scenes in which Hallie and Annie appeared together, the film's director, Nancy Meyers, filmed Lindsay playing the roles in separate **takes**. There still was a stand-in, but Lindsay's various performances were digitally spliced over the stand-in through the use of computer editing.

Along with being technically innovative, this arrangement demanded some complicated acting from Lindsay. She had to deliver a line as Annie, and then later react to that same line as Hallie. Meyers was thrilled that Lindsay successfully pulled it off. "It was an amazing feat," the producer told *Vanity Fair*.

The Parent Trap was an enormously successful movie, earning $92 million at the box office. Lindsay's performance also received praise from film critics. Writing in the *Los Angeles Times*, Kenneth Turan said,

> **❝ *The Parent Trap* can't be imagined without its 11-year-old redheaded star, Lindsay Lohan. Her bright spirit and impish smile make for an immensely likable young person we take to our hearts almost at once. Lohan's the soul of this film as much as Hayley Mills was of the original, and, aided by a gift for accent and considerably improved technology, she is more adept than her predecessor at creating two distinct personalities for the unknowing twin sisters who meet at Camp Walden in Moose Lake, Maine. ❞**

High School Cheerleader

After filming *The Parent Trap*, Lindsay accepted a few brief acting jobs. She was cast in *Life-Size*, a *Wonderful World of Disney* TV movie that was shown in 2000. In the film, her character, Casey Stuart, finds a book of magic and uses it to conjure up a new wife for her father, whose wife has recently died. Instead, the magic spell backfires and Casey brings to life a doll named Eve, played by supermodel Tyra Banks. Lindsay's work in this movie later led to another Disney TV movie role, *Get a Clue*. In that production, Lindsay played a high school newspaper reporter who sniffs out a mystery when one of her teachers disappears.

In between *Life-Size* and *Get a Clue*, Lindsay accepted a role on the TV comedy *Bette*, starring pop star Bette Midler. Lindsay helped make the **pilot**, but then dropped out when the producers opted to film the series in Los Angeles instead of New York. She had decided against

In 2001, when this photo was taken, Lindsay had decided to take a break from acting and focus on high school. She enjoyed doing many of the things that ordinary teenagers do, including hanging out with friends and participating in school activities. She was offered many acting jobs, though, and eventually she would decide to go back to work.

doing the show in Los Angeles because she was still going to school, and didn't want to uproot her life to move to the West Coast. It later proved a smart move, as *Bette* only garnered a small audience and lasted just a few episodes before it was canceled.

By 2001 Lindsay had decided to take a break from performing and simply wanted to recapture some of the childhood that she left behind for her acting career. She concentrated on her studies at Calhoun High School in Merrick. In some ways, things returned to normal. She was simply known to her school friends as "Linds," spending her junior year playing on the basketball and soccer teams and performing on the cheerleading squad.

Nevertheless, there was no getting around the fact that Lindsay was not just another student at Calhoun High. *The Parent Trap* had established her as one of Hollywood's brightest up-and-coming stars. The calls were coming in from the producers, and Lindsay would realize that she could only ignore their offers for movie roles for so long.

Jamie Lee Curtis (right) appears with Lindsay at a party promoting their 2003 film *Freaky Friday*. Like *The Parent Trap*, *Freaky Friday* was a remake of another classic Disney film, with Lindsay in the role originally played by Jodie Foster. The 2003 movie also starred Chad Michael Murray and Mark Harmon.

3

Out of Control

It was Disney studios that convinced Lindsay to leave the normal high school life behind and appear in another movie. This time, she would star in *Freaky Friday*, a story about a mother and daughter who swap bodies for a day so they can see life through each other's eyes.

By now, Lindsay was anxious to get back into acting. Although she was enjoying her life at Calhoun High School, she saw how the careers of other actresses her age were advancing. In taking Disney's offer, she had to drop out of school (she eventually received her high school diploma with the help of tutors).

Freaky Friday was originally released in 1976 and starred Jodie Foster. In the new version of *Freaky Friday*, Lindsay plays 15-year-old Anna, the role Foster had played in the original film, and Jamie Lee Curtis plays the role of her mother Tess. Anna is a young rocker whose band, Pink Slip, is about to get its big break, while Tess, a **psychologist**, is about to remarry. However, the plans of both Anna and Tess are jinxed when a spell causes them to switch each other's bodies. Tess joins her daughter's rock band while Anna takes her mother's place as a psychologist. Although its plot is hardly serious, this light comedy required strong acting performances from Lindsay and Curtis. Since the two characters switch bodies, Lindsay and Curtis had to learn how to mimic each other's mannerisms, movements, and voice patterns.

Remembering the challenges she overcame with *The Parent Trap*, Lindsay had experience to draw from in playing Anna. The film's director, Mark Waters, also provided Lindsay and Curtis with direction in preparing for their roles. He videotaped each actress delivering her lines, then showed Lindsay and Curtis the tapes so they could study each other's movements and voices. Said Lindsay,

"It kind of helped [me] figure out little gestures that Jamie would do in a scene, and it would help me become more like her character. It worked out for the better for us."

Winning Back the Critics

Lindsay received good reviews for her work in *Freaky Friday*. In the *Chicago Sun-Times*, movie critic Roger Ebert said, "Lindsay Lohan . . . has that Jodie Foster sort of seriousness and intense focus beneath her teenage persona."

But perhaps Lindsay's streak of positive reviews had to end some-time, because the critics were less appreciative of her next movie, *Confessions of a Teenage Drama Queen*. In the film, which was released in 2004 and based on the young-adult novel of the same name by Dyan Sheldon, Lindsay portrays a high school student suddenly forced to move to the suburbs, where she finds that she is no longer as popular as she was at her old school. The story follows her character, Lola, as she tries to thwart competitors looking to claim the position of most popular girl. Writing in the *Chicago Tribune*, critic Robert K. Elder called Lindsay's performance "wooden," and added that her character was not consistent with the type of personality fans had grown accustomed to in Lindsay's previous movies:

"We like our teen rebels (even Disney teen rebels) to be brash, a tad bratty and even roguish—but not self-absorbed to the point of alienation. Though still a promising star, Lohan will have to do a little penance before she's forgiven for *Confessions*."

Lola Cep, the character Lindsay played in the 2004 film *Confessions of a Teenage Drama Queen*, is similar in some ways to her *Mean Girls* character Cady Heron. Like Cady, Lola is the new girl in town and winds up in a conflict with the school's most popular girl. *Confessions* was Lindsay's first film that was not a remake.

The setback was short, because just a few months later Lindsay regained her status with the critically acclaimed *Mean Girls*. She followed up that performance the following year with another starring role, appearing in *Herbie: Fully Loaded*. This was part of a series of

Members of the cast and crew of *Herbie: Fully Loaded*, including Lindsay (seated, second from right), watch some of that day's filmed scenes being played back on small monitors. The film was very successful, earning more than $144 million, and Lindsay won a 2006 Kids' Choice Award as Favorite Female Actress for her portrayal of Maggie Peyton.

Disney films featuring a Volkswagen Beetle with a mind of its own. While this comedy was not far removed from the subject matter of Lindsay's earlier films, none of those films had approached the box office total of *Herbie*, over $144 million.

The commercial success of the film showed that Lindsay was now an established Hollywood actress whose presence in a film could virtually guarantee a hit for the studio. As an added bonus, she was now old enough to play more adult roles. That kind of recognition and range meant that she could start commanding fees of some $7 million per movie.

Tabloid Target

Now aged 18 and an established Hollywood actress, Lindsay began living the independent life. She decided to share an apartment with TV actress Raven-Symone. She also become more serious about relationships and started dating. It did not take long for gossip-hungry tabloid journalists to begin tracking her every move. She was photographed at any number of Hollywood nightspots—dancing and drinking, even though she was not old enough to have alcohol. Rumors began springing up about the men in her life, and stories included the names of such heartthrobs as pop singer Aaron Carter, actor Colin Farrell, and Talan Torriero, star of the MTV reality show *Laguna Beach*. The accounts of her love life were so numerous that *People* magazine eventually ran a feature story reporting the names of some 20 singers, actors, and other performers who had supposedly been involved with Lindsay.

Among this long list of male candidates, one star's name began popping up more than any other. He was Wilmer Valderrama, the comic actor known as Fez on the hit TV comedy *That '70s Show*. Lindsay and Valderrama spent time with each other during much of 2004. Soon she left the apartment she shared with Raven-Symone and moved in with Valderrama. Describing her relationship with him to *Rolling Stone*, Lindsay said,

"We've become really, really good friends. I love him to death. He's a great guy. He's been there for me. . . . We'll see what happens. If this matures into a serious relationship, he'll be my first real boyfriend. But I don't know. I'm only 18. I want to have fun."

The paparazzi snapped this shot of Lindsay and a boyfriend outside of a nightclub. After she moved into an apartment of her own, Lindsay began to gain a reputation as a wild partier and was linked romantically with a number of eligible young bachelors. Eventually she began a serious relationship with actor Wilmer Valderrama.

Spat with Hilary Duff

If the tabloids couldn't get enough of Lindsay's romantic life, she soon provided the gossip columnists with even more juicy details for their readers. It didn't take long for the papers to uncover a spat between Lindsay and actress Hilary Duff, both of whom had dated Aaron Carter in 2002. In fact, things between the two starlets got nasty in 2003 when Carter showed up at the premiere of *Freaky Friday* with Duff on his arm. A few months later, Lindsay and Duff encountered each other again at the premiere of Duff's movie, *Cheaper by the Dozen.* By now, Lindsay had already started dating Valderrama but rumors surfaced suggesting that Carter had been seeing Duff at the same time he was dating Lindsay.

News of the spat was reported in the tabloids for months, where the two actresses traded nasty comments about one another. Lindsay told *USA Today*,

> **Things get dragged on by the public because people are interested in making things bigger than they are, but it should be let go. It's immature. It's silly. I'm sure she doesn't like me for whatever her reasons are, but I have no problem with her. If she has a problem with me, she should talk to me about it.**

At this point, though, the two movie stars were hardly on speaking terms. In an interview with the press, Duff said, "I think I've met her, maybe, twice. It's like every single time I see her, she starts talking bad about me."

And then, in 2004, Duff released an album, titled *Hilary Duff*, in which she included the song "Haters." The **lyrics** of the song did not mention Lindsay by name, but it was clear to Hollywood insiders that Duff had taken direct aim at her rival. The song included the lyrics,

> **You're the queen of superficiality**
> **Keep your lies out of my reality. . . .**
> **You say your boyfriend's sweet and kind**
> **But you've still got your eyes on mine.**

After months of trading gossip and rumors about one another in the tabloid newspapers, Lindsay finally had enough. She decided to call Duff and settle the fight. Later, she told a reporter for the *London Sunday Times*,

> **"Eurgh, it was so stupid! And I was like, 'We have a lot of friends in L.A., let's just be cool so if we see each other everything's fine.' I don't wanna have fights with people."**

Nonstop Party

Lindsay's personal problems took a heavy toll on her relationship with Valderrama, and the couple broke up in fall 2004. Soon after they split, her life spiraled into a nonstop, out-of-control party. Each night, she hit the nightclubs in Hollywood. Even though she still was not old enough to drink legally, she found a way to party until dawn.

Lindsay's family problems had made her life even more complicated. Her father, who had gotten out of prison, was back in trouble with the law. In the summer of 2004 he had been arrested for attacking his brother-in-law with a shoe. A month later, he assaulted a trash collector on a New York City street.

Dina Lohan was so frightened of him that she won a court order prohibiting Michael from having contact with family members, which he violated by attending his son Dakota's soccer game. Dina immediate called the police, and the officers who arrived to the scene had to forcibly restrain Michael. Soon, he was back in prison. It had all been reported by the tabloids, and Lindsay now had to deal with her father's name next to her own in the headlines.

A breakup with a boyfriend. An out-of-control father. A public feud with Hilary Duff. A social life run ragged by nonstop drinking and clubbing. In the midst of all this personal chaos, Lindsay was weighed down by a busy movie-making schedule along with preparations to record her first album.

Losing Weight

The tabloid reporters and photographers continued to hound Lindsay in 2005. Looking at the dozens of published photographs, Hollywood insiders as well as her fans couldn't help noticing that she seemed to be losing weight. Fresh rumors swirled around Lindsay, suggesting that she suffered from an eating disorder known as **bulimia**. Similar to **anorexia nervosa**, girls who suffer from bulimia have a desire to lose

In 2003 and 2004 a feud developed between Lindsay and another Disney star, singer and actress Hilary Duff, shown here performing during a concert. Singer Aaron Carter caused the rivalry when he broke up with Lindsay to date Hilary. The two celebrities traded nasty comments in the tabloids for months.

Lindsay blows a kiss to reporters and photographers while walking down the red carpet at a Hollywood event. Photos like this one taken of Lindsay in 2005 showed that she had lost a great deal of weight. The star's changing appearance led many of Lindsay's friends to worry that she might have an eating disorder.

weight at any cost. Bulimics and anorexics will even risk their lives to lose weight by taking such drastic steps as dieting to the point of starvation or forcing themselves to vomit after each meal. At first, Lindsay vigorously denied the rumors. In an interview with *Cosmopolitan* magazine in 2006, she said,

> **"I'm not bulimic. . . . I wasn't happy, and I was going through a lot of personal things. I wasn't eating right. Sometimes I just wouldn't eat, I think. I was really worn out and exhausted."**

Still, Lindsay refused to give up the Hollywood party scene. In addition to breaking the law as an underage drinker, she was proving that she could not control herself under the influence of alcohol.

Meanwhile, the tabloids were following her at every turn, which had horrible consequences. In October 2005, while eluding a nearby reporter she crashed her Mercedes-Benz on a busy Los Angeles street, cracking her wrist. No sooner was she out of the car and nursing her injury when she saw photographers surround the wreck.

As the attention on Lindsay by the tabloids and gossip columnists intensified, it became painfully clear to the young star that the public was learning a lot about her that she had hoped she could keep secret.

Lindsay has always been interested in a singing career. By 2004, when her first album, *Speak*, was released, she had already recorded songs for her movies *Freaky Friday* and *Confessions of a Teenage Drama Queen*. Although none of the singles from the album hit the Billboard charts, *Speak* eventually sold more than a million copies.

4

New Challenges, Old Troubles

Through the decades the entertainment world has been dazzled by what have been called "triple threats," female stars who can act, sing, and dance. During recent decades, Jennifer Lopez and Madonna tore up both the music charts and the silver screen. During the 1960s and 1970s one performer, Ann-Margret, set the triple-threat standard long before these stars.

Star of famous musical films like *Bye Bye Birdie* and *Viva Las Vegas*, Ann-Margret was a main inspiration for Lindsay as she launched her recording career. While studying the career of her idol, Lindsay resolved to expand her appeal as an entertainer beyond the comedic roles she had been accepting in films.

Lindsay released her first album in 2004. Titled *Speak*, the pop-rock album was applauded by critics and embraced by her fans. She wrote the lyrics for about half the songs on the album and worked hard to promote the record, appearing on several radio and TV shows to perform tracks from the disc. Lindsay explained her newfound passion in an interview with *Billboard* magazine. She said,

> **"I am sure people don't expect me to be really singing. I know they're saying things like, 'Oh, she's just another actress-turned-singer.' But I love exploring other areas in entertainment. I love triple threats like Ann-Margret—an actress, dancer and singer."**

Big Disappointment

Lindsay managed to work as a singer while keeping a busy acting schedule. She even recorded some of the album in the midst of filming *Herbie: Fully Loaded*. Shortly after the album's release, Lindsay began work on another movie, *Just My Luck*. Costarring Chris Pine, this romantic comedy tells the story of a supernatural change of luck after the world's luckiest woman, Ashley Albright, kisses the world's unluckiest man, Jake Hardin, at a masquerade ball.

Despite having what some thought a clever premise, *Just My Luck* flopped at the box office. The movie earned a mere $30 million in the United States and other countries—a disappointment for the studio considering Lindsay's star reputation. Critics panned the story's plot as well as Lindsay's performance. A review in *People* magazine said,

> **"It's a cardboard-thin plot boasting no real laughs. Lohan is trying her hardest to be wacky and the strain shows. Hers are mighty slight shoulders upon which to dump the entire weight of a movie."**

A Great Role

It seemed that Lindsay got the message. She became much more careful in the film roles she selected, opting instead for more adult movies that were a step above the light, whimsical comedies for

After finishing *Herbie: Fully Loaded*, Lindsay starred in the romantic comedy *Just My Luck*. In an interview, she described the film as "a little bit of an over-the-top comedy, but it's funny and it's cute and it's silly." For making the film, Lindsay earned $7.5 million—her biggest paycheck to that point.

which she had gained her fame. She also resolved to work with more talented directors, so when the veteran director Robert Altman offered her a role in his next project, *A Prairie Home Companion*, she quickly accepted.

For years, Altman had been one of the movie industry's top directors. His best-known films include *MASH* and *Gosford Park*, both of which won Academy Awards. Like many of Altman's films, *A Prairie Home Companion* featured an impressive **ensemble** cast, which meant Lindsay had the unique opportunity to work with actors like two-time Academy

Award–winner Meryl Streep as well as Lily Tomlin, Woody Harrelson, Kevin Kline, and Tommy Lee Jones. Also appearing in the film as himself was Garrison Keillor, the creator and host of the weekly radio variety show on which the film was based. Playing the role of Lola Johnson, a **suicidal** young poet and singer who is estranged from her father, Lindsay accompanies her mother, a folk singer, to a taping of the variety show.

Lindsay said that playing Lola turned out to be one of the most difficult roles in her life, partly because the character's pain about her father resembled her own. In the interview with *Vanity Fair*, she remembered her experience filming the movie:

> **"I was *scared*. Meryl [and Lily] are singing this emotional song and I'm chiming in. And I don't have a father in the movie, I don't really know my dad. And [Lola's] talking about the dad and she starts singing, and I just started to cry in the scene when we were improvising. . . . That was the first day of shooting. . . . They were so nice to me and kind, and I was so proud of myself. That changed me a lot, I guess."**

Many movie critics were also delighted with her acting. When *A Prairie Home Companion* was released in 2006, the film garnered mixed reviews, but critics praised Lindsay and said that her performance stood out among the large ensemble cast.

Altman was at first hesitant to use Lindsay, doubting that she could shed her reputation as a comic actress for the darker role of a young woman contemplating suicide. But she soon won him over and the two became close friends during the production. David Levy, one of the producers of *A Prairie Home Companion*, explained to *Newsday* that the film marked a new direction for Lindsay's career. He said,

> **"Lindsay wanted to move into more adult projects. On *Prairie*, we had the part of a young girl we hadn't cast and her 'people,' as we say, came to us. She's great. She wanted to be part of a film where she wasn't in every scene. It moves her away from the kid pictures."**

Lindsay braves the paparazzi to make a guest appearance at *The Late Show with David Letterman* **in New York City to promote her new movie** *A Prairie Home Companion.* **Moving away from her typical comic roles, Lindsay's portrayal of the suicidal Lola marked a turning point in her acting career.**

A great opportunity for professional growth came in 2006, when award-winning director Robert Altman invited Lindsay to join the all-star ensemble cast of his film *A Prairie Home Companion*. Here Garrison Keillor watches Lindsay performs with Meryl Streep. Other talented actors who appeared in the comedy included Lily Tomlin, Kevin Kline, Woody Harrelson, Virginia Madsen, and Tommy Lee Jones.

Exhausted

After completing *A Prairie Home Companion* in 2005, Lindsay looked back on two busy and productive years. In 2004, she filmed two movies along with recording her album. In addition to filming *A*

Prairie Home Companion the following year, she also guest hosted *Saturday Night Live* for a second time. However, even as her career continued to move forward, her lifestyle was holding her back. A hectic schedule and constant partying made for a destructive mix and took a physical toll on Lindsay.

During production of *Herbie: Fully Loaded*, Lindsay's body suddenly shut down. She was briefly hospitalized for exhaustion, stalling production of the film for three days. She told *Vanity Fair*,

> **"I started to get really bad head pains, to the point where I was shaking in my trailer. I got a fever of 102. . . . I started getting these shooting head pains, where I would wake up in the middle of the night. I kid you not, I was lying in that bed and I never heard someone scream so loud. . . . [T]he pains were so intense in my head, like someone was stabbing me in the head."**

Always hungry for a story about Lindsay, the tabloid press started snooping around as soon as they received word about her hospitalization. They connected her poor health with her partying, and published stories of her nights out with some of the biggest stars in town, including actresses Mary-Kate and Ashley Olsen, Paris Hilton, and Nicole Richie.

Facing the Facts

It was on the night of Lindsay's second stint as *Saturday Night Live* guest host that she was confronted with yet another physical problem that was prime tabloid fodder: her declining weight. At the time, *Mean Girls* was hitting the theaters, and Lindsay had agreed to promote the film by taking the guest host slot. She had been excited to have another opportunity to work with her *Mean Girls* costar Tina Fey. However, when Lindsay showed up for rehearsals, it was clear to Fey and the show's producer, Lorne Michaels, that she had lost a lot of weight and was suffering from an eating disorder.

As she had dismissed questions about her weight to the tabloids, Lindsay denied the accusations from Fey and Michaels. But they held fast and urged her to acknowledge her problem. Recalling the meeting to *Vanity Fair*, Lindsay said,

Rumors about Lindsay's partying with some of the hottest young stars in Hollywood, including Mary-Kate and Ashley Olsen, began to appear in tabloids during 2004. (Lindsay was pictured with Mary-Kate and Ashley on the cover of *Vanity Fair*'s July 2003 issue—she appears on the far right, while the twins are second and third from left.)

❝They sat me down, literally before I was going to do the show, and they said, 'You need to take care of yourself. We care about you too much, and we've seen too many people do this, and you're talented,' and I just started bawling. I knew I had a problem and I couldn't admit it. . . . I saw that [*Saturday Night Live*] after I did it. My arms were disgusting. I had no arms.❞

Despite the prodding from Michaels and Fey, Lindsay still had no intentions of slowing down or giving up the party life. During production for *Georgia Rule*, which began in the summer of 2006, Lindsay continued to live up to her reputation as the reckless party girl. She spent much of her time in the clubs, somehow squeezing time for drinking and dancing between the hours on the movie set.

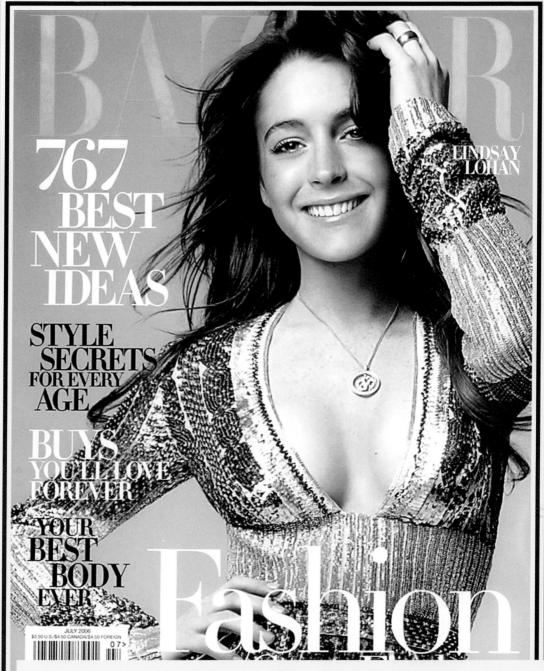

767 BEST NEW IDEAS

STYLE SECRETS FOR EVERY AGE

BUYS YOU'LL LOVE FOREVER

YOUR BEST BODY EVER

LINDSAY LOHAN

BAZAAR

Fashion

JULY 2006
$3.50 U.S./$4.50 CANADA/$4.50 FOREIGN

0 7 >

For Lindsay 2006 was another busy year and she continued to run at top speed—appearing in three films (*Just My Luck, A Prairie Home Companion*, and *Bobby*) and working on a fourth (*Georgia Rule*). Nonetheless, she still found time to pose for the July cover of *Harpers Bazaar*, and to do some serious partying.

A member of the paparazzi captured this shot of Lindsay walking down a street alone. By 2006 the young actress was a constant target of photographers, and her wild behavior was often reported in the tabloids. Lindsay's late-night schedule caused her to miss work, which led to an angry rebuke from the producer of her film *Georgia Rule*.

Georgia Rule, released in 2007, is a drama about an uncontrollable young woman named Rachel, played by Lindsay, who learns compassion, respect, and self-control once she moves in with her grandmother. The movie gave Lindsay another opportunity to work with accomplished actors, including two-time Academy Award–winner Jane Fonda, playing Rachel's grandmother, and TV actress Felicity Huffman, playing Rachel's mother.

More Embarrassment

The filming of the movie did not proceed smoothly. Lindsay often called in sick, claiming exhaustion. Fed up with the excuses, the film's producer, James G. Robinson, decide to issue a warning to the actress. He wrote Lindsay a letter demanding that she live up to her obligations to the movie.

Robinson's letter was leaked to the tabloid newspapers, and its subsequent publication only added to Lindsay's public embarrassments over the past several months. Robinson not only mentioned Lindsay's failure to make it to the set, but also accused her of showing more interest in going to parties and nightclubs than in giving a good performance. He wrote,

> **"Since the commencement of principal photography of *Georgia Rule*, you have frequently failed to arrive on time to the set. . . . We are well aware that your ongoing all night heavy partying is the real reason for your so called 'exhaustion.' We refuse to accept bogus excuses for your behavior. . . . [Y]our actions on *Georgia Rule* have been discourteous, irresponsible and unprofessional. You have acted like a spoiled child . . ."**

After receiving the rebuke from Robinson, Lindsay made good on her commitments to *Georgia Rule*. In addition to showing up on time on a regular basis, she also apologized to the cast and crew members for her poor behavior.

Although she had owned up to her mistakes on this most recent project, it was still clear Lindsay desperately needed to make more changes. Her drinking was out of control. Sadly, there would more embarrassing public displays of drunkenness before she finally realized that it was time to seek help and take control of her life.

In 2007 Lindsay acknowledged that her partying had become a problem, joining Alcoholics Anonymous and entering a rehab program. She released a statement to the media that said, "I have made a proactive decision to take care of my personal health. I appreciate your well wishes and ask that you please respect my privacy at this time."

5

Road to Recovery

Wonderland Center in Los Angeles could easily be mistaken for a resort hotel. Visitors have access to two swimming pools, horseback riding, hiking trails, yoga classes, and a gym. While the center has its share of luxuries, it primarily serves as a rehabilitation center. It was here that Lindsay made a serious commitment toward shaking her drinking habit.

Lindsay entered rehab on January 17, 2007. Just weeks before, she had acknowledged her drinking problem by disclosing to reporters that she had been attending meetings of Alcoholics Anonymous (AA). Members of AA go to regular meetings to receive encouragement by other members as they attempt to stay clear of abusing alcohol. In this tight-knit community, the AA member receives support from a type of **mentor** called a sponsor, who provides a shoulder to lean on. But even though the sponsor serves as a major support, ultimately the alcoholic must decide whether to stop drinking for good.

While there is no question that joining AA was a positive step for Lindsay, it soon became clear that she needed a much stronger form of treatment. Despite the promises she was making at AA meetings, she continued to drink and many of her exploits continued to end up in the pages of the tabloids.

Public Ridicule

A month before moving into the Wonderland Center, Lindsay attended a dinner sponsored by *GQ* magazine. While attending the party, she noticed that one of her former assistants, Lindsay Ratowsky, had attended the event with her new boss, actress Jessica Biel. Evidently, Lindsay had had a falling out with Ratowsky, and when she saw her at the *GQ* dinner, she exploded. According to the magazine *Us Weekly*, she barked,

> **"How dare you let her in here! I am suing her! This is supposed to be for the crème de la crème and you let her in when I am suing her. I am going to leave unless you kick her out!"**

Us Weekly also reported that Lindsay's rage was fueled by **champagne**, and that she had lost her temper in front of respectable company like Hollywood stars Ben Affleck and Leonardo DiCaprio as well as former vice president Al Gore. Meanwhile, the tabloids were also reporting that Lindsay's friendship with goth rocker Marilyn Manson had contributed to the recent breakup of the singer's marriage.

The blow-up at the *GQ* dinner and the news about Manson's marital woes broke right after Lindsay had suffered yet another public blunder. The mistake this time was a poorly written e-mail expressing condolences to the family of *A Prairie Home Companion* director Robert Altman, who died in November 2006. Lindsay had grown close to Altman during the production of the film and was devastated when he died.

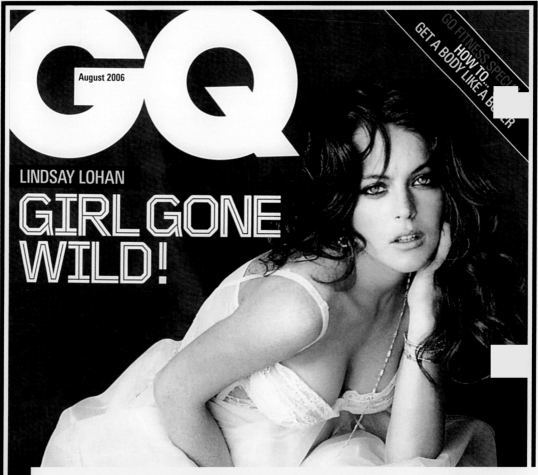

August 2006

GQ

GQ FITNESS SPECIAL
HOW TO...
GET A BODY LIKE A BOXER

LINDSAY LOHAN

GIRL GONE WILD!

Lindsay appears on the cover of *GQ* magazine's August 2006 issue. Later that year Lindsay's angry tantrum at a dinner party sponsored by *GQ* resulted in more bad publicity for the young star. This was one of several embarrassing incidents that may have contributed to Lindsay's decision to enter rehab early in 2007.

Lindsay's message was heartfelt, yet was also filled with misspellings and numerous errors in grammar. The e-mail fell into the hands of a columnist for the *Los Angeles Times*, who published it and called it "alarmingly incoherent." Lindsay's **publicist** later said that the actress had dashed it off without giving much thought to how the message was worded; nevertheless, once again Lindsay found herself the subject of public ridicule in the press.

Critical Praise

While the media always seemed to focus on Lindsay's most embarrassing public moments, her work as an entertainer was nevertheless earning critical praise. In late 2005, she released her second album, *A Little More Personal (Raw)*. As Lindsay demonstrated with her recent films, this album makes clear her intention to leave her familiar image as a teenage star far behind.

The album's songs concentrate on deep emotions such as love and loneliness and examine a young woman's entry into adulthood. In her *Entertainment Weekly* review, music critic Leah Greenblatt said,

> **"Lindsay may no longer be on the edge of 17, but being 19, troubled, and ridiculously famous can cut pretty deep, so props to her for letting us see her bleed—just a little."**

In 2006 Lohan returned to acting to appear in her second ensemble film. The movie, titled *Bobby*, tells the story of a day in the lives of a number of characters who arrive at the Ambassador Hotel in Los Angeles on June 4, 1968, a day before the assassination of the famed U.S. senator Robert F. Kennedy.

That evening the Ambassador hosted the victory party for Kennedy, a candidate for president who had won the California **primary** earlier that day. At the party in the hotel ballroom, as Kennedy was surrounded by cheering fans, an assassin stepped out of the crowd and shot the senator, who died in a hospital the following day.

The film featured roles for more than 20 of Hollywood's top actors and actresses, including Demi Moore, Sharon Stone, Elijah Wood, Ashton Kutcher, Heather Graham, and Helen Hunt. In the film, Lohan played the role of Diane, a young woman who has agreed to marry a man she hardly knows because she is aware his marriage status will exempt him from the **draft**. Critic Ann Hornaday observed in the *Washington Post* how Lohan's role, though small, lent profound meaning to the picture. She wrote,

> **"In Bobby, [the] generation is most effectively embodied by a character named Diane (Lindsay Lohan), who has come to the Ambassador to marry a young man she knows only vaguely.... Jittery and sad**

A scene from the 2006 film *Bobby*, which was a fictional account of the day presidential candidate Robert F. Kennedy was assassinated in 1968. Lindsay's character, Diane Huber, is a girl who decides to marry her boyfriend William Avary (played by Elijah Wood) so that he can avoid military service in Vietnam.

(her parents are boycotting the ceremony), she's also fired by the moral certainty that she's saving a life. When she explains what she's doing to a manicurist played by Sharon Stone, the unspoken wisdom between the two women is ... quietly electrifying.**"**

Rehabilitating

Her performance in *Bobby* proved that Lindsay could still impress the critics, but in January 2007, she recognized that her well-being was more important than any acting accomplishment. At the Wonderland Center, Lindsay received counseling from substance abuse experts on how to resist the temptation to drink. Although she was permitted to leave the center during the day to work on a new film, she was required to return each night where the counselors kept a close watch on her for the full 30 days of her treatment program.

A few days after entering rehab, a reporter for *OK! Magazine* reached her by telephone. Lindsay told the reporter that she had adjusted well to life at the center and was spending her nights watching TV. She told the reporter,

> **"I'm doing so great. I'm fine, nothing to worry about. Thank you so much for checking in, I do appreciate it. I'm actually watching *American Idol* at the moment and laughing so hard!"**

Alcoholism is a serious disease, and Lindsay will have to overcome many obstacles to shake her habit for good. Her acting and singing career could very well help her to stay focused. With a newfound dedication to acting, she landed another challenging role near the end of 2006 in the thriller *I Know Who Killed Me*. In the film, which was released in 2007, Lindsay plays a young woman who escapes from a **serial killer**.

Because she was required to stay at the Wonderland Center during her rehabilitation, Lindsay she could not attend the premiere of her film, *Chapter 27*, when it debuted at the Sundance Film Festival in January 2007. In that drama, Lindsay plays the girlfriend of Mark David Chapman, the man who murdered rock icon John Lennon. Another film project she began in 2007 was *The Best Time of Our Lives*, in which she plays the wife of Welsh poet Dylan Thomas. In addition, according to *Life & Style* magazine, she has expressed interest in playing rock signer Stevie Nicks in a biography, and may even be one of the film's producers.

There is no doubt she has a busy film and singing career ahead of her, but keeping her position as one of Hollywood's biggest stars will depend on how well Lindsay can handle her alcohol dependence and stay away from the Hollywood party scene.

Helping Others

Lindsay is aware that she is a celebrity with a large following, and that she has a responsibility to be a model for her fans—particularly young

Work on the film *I Know Who Killed Me* was halted when Lindsay entered a rehab program in January 2007. The movie was finished after she completed the program a month later. *I Know Who Killed Me* is a thriller in which Lindsay's character must escape from a serial killer.

girls. To help set that good example, she has become active in a number of charitable causes, including the Carol M. Baldwin Breast Cancer Foundation, which was started by three brothers of the famous acting family—Alec, Stephen, and William—and other relatives to help find a cure for breast cancer.

Another charity in which Lindsay is involved is Save the Children, which raises money to provide health care, food, and other necessities

Lindsay autographs a jacket that will be auctioned off for charity at the 2005 Young Hollywood Awards in Los Angeles. Over the years Lindsay has been involved with a number of charities, and has helped to raise money for breast cancer research, to feed poor children, and to help people living with the disease cerebral palsy.

of life to children who live in poverty in the United States and foreign countries. She has also worked with Dream Come True, which provides vacations and other special gifts to ill children, and the United Cerebral Palsy Foundation, which raises money for medical researchers looking to find a cure for cerebral palsy, a disability that robs victims of their muscular function.

Lindsay's newfound interest in public service illustrates her recent growth as an individual. Reflecting on the satisfaction she has felt in helping others, she told *Vanity Fair,*

> **"[D]oing great things makes me want to do even better things. I want to do things that make me feel good, and work with charities and see the positive side of things. With the position that I've kind of come into I'm in a place where I can really make an impact on people and really help girls that are, you know, people with anorexia, people that aren't in good relationships . . . people that don't get along with their parents. I can change that a little bit."**

Hardly the expressions of a high school "teenage drama queen." Now a Hollywood veteran and someone who has endured the rough times, Lindsay has graduated from adolescence with plenty of personal wisdom to share.

1986   Lindsay Dee Lohan is born July 2 on Long Island, New York.

1989   Begins modeling in print advertising and acting in TV commercials.

1992   Appears in a skit on *Late Night with David Letterman*.

1996   Lands a role in the TV soap opera *Another World*.

1997   Wins dual parts of twin characters in *The Parent Trap* and begins filming in England and California.

1998   Becomes bona-fide star with commercial success of *The Parent Trap*.

1999   Wins Youth In Film Young Artist Award for Best Performance by a Leading Young Actress in *The Parent Trap*.

2000   Stars in *Life-Size*, a made-for-TV movie.

Appears in the pilot episode of the television show *Bette*.

2001   Takes a brief break from acting and attends a regular high school.

2002   Stars in the TV movie *Get a Clue*.

2003   Drops out of Calhoun High School on Long Island to film *Freaky Friday*.

Feuds with Hilary Duff over the rival actress's relationship with Lohan's former boyfriend, singer Aaron Carter.

2004   Stars in *Mean Girls* and *Confessions of a Teenage Drama Queen*.

Starts dating TV sitcom actor Wilmer Valderrama.

Releases first album, *Speak*.

Is hospitalized for exhaustion.

Stars as guest host on *Saturday Night Live*.

2005 Breaks up with Valderrama.

Stars in *Herbie: Fully Loaded*.

Crashes her car while being followed by paparazzi.

Releases her second album, *A Little More Personal (Raw)*.

Makes second appearance as guest host on *Saturday Night Live*.

2006 Plays roles in films *A Prairie Home Companion*, *Chapter 27*, *Bobby*, and *Georgia Rule*.

During shooting of *Georgia Rule* is warned that her nonstop partying is stalling production.

Acknowledges drinking problem by joining Alcoholics Anonymous.

2007 Enters an addiction rehabilitation center in Los Angeles, California.

Begins filming *I Know Who Killed Me*.

ACCOMPLISHMENTS & AWARDS

Movies

1998 *The Parent Trap*

2000 *Life-Size* (made for TV)

2002 *Get a Clue* (made for TV)

2003 *Freaky Friday*

2004 *Confessions of a Teenage Drama Queen*
Mean Girls

2005 *Herbie: Fully Loaded*

2006 *Just My Luck*
A Prairie Home Companion
Bobby

2007 *Chapter 27*
Georgia Rule
I Know Who Killed Me

2008 *The Best Time of Our Lives*

Albums

2004 *Speak*

2005 *A Little More Personal (Raw)*

Television

1992 *Late Night with David Letterman*

2004 *MTV Movie Awards*
Saturday Night Live

2005 *Saturday Night Live*

Awards

1998 Nominated for *Hollywood Reporter* Young Star Award for Best Performance by a Young Actress in a Comedy for *The Parent Trap*

1999 Nominated for Blockbuster Entertainment Award for Favorite Female Newcomer for *The Parent Trap*

2004   Nominated for Saturn Award by the Academy of Science Fiction, Fantasy and Horror Films for Best Performance by a Younger Actor for *Freaky Friday*

Won MTV Movie Award for Breakthrough Female Performance for *Freaky Friday*

Won Teen Choice Awards for Female Breakout Movie Star, Movie Actress in a Comedy for *Mean Girls*

2005   Nominated by the Broadcast Film Critics Association for Best Young Actress for *Mean Girls*

Nominated for Kids' Choice Blimp Award for Favorite Movie Actress for *Mean Girls*

Won MTV Movie Award for Best Female Performance for *Mean Girls*

Nominated for Teen Choice Award for Movie Actress in a Comedy for *Herbie: Fully Loaded*

2006   Shared nomination for Independent Feature Project Gotham Award for Best Ensemble Cast for *A Prairie Home Companion*

Won Hollywood Film Festival Breakthrough Actress Award and Shared Award for Ensemble of the Year for *Bobby*

Won Kids' Choice Blimp Award for Favorite Movie Actress for *Herbie: Fully Loaded*

Shared nomination for Screen Actors Guild Award for Outstanding Performance by a Cast in a Motion Picture for *Bobby*

Nominated for Teen Choice Award for Movie Actress in a Comedy for *Just My Luck*

Books

Boone, Mary. *Lindsay Lohan: A Star on the Rise.* Chicago: Triumph Entertainment, 2004.

Brown, Lauren. *Lindsay Lohan: The "It" Girl Next Door.* New York: Simon Spotlight, 2004.

Johns, Michael-Anne. *Hangin' with Lindsay Lohan.* New York: Scholastic, 2004.

Rodgers, Mary. *Freaky Friday.* New York: Avon Books, 2003.

Tracy, Kathleen. *Lindsay Lohan.* Hockessin, Del.: Mitchell Lane Publishers, 2005.

Web Sites

http://prairiehome.publicradio.org

Web site for the National Public Radio program *A Prairie Home Companion.* Visitors can listen to audio highlights from the show, download photos of the show's personalities, read humorous stories and poems submitted by listeners, and watch the trailer for the film version that featured Lindsay Lohan.

www.alcoholics-anonymous.org

Web site for Alcoholics Anonymous describes the activities of the organization, which includes some 2 million members in 140 countries. AA works with alcoholics by helping them recognize their addictions and providing support.

www.llrocks.com

Lindsay Lohan's official Web site; visitors can find a brief biography of the actress, descriptions of her movies, photographs of Lohan, and news about her charitable work.

www.meangirls.com

The Web site for the movie *Mean Girls* features photos from the film, interviews with the director and actors, interactive games, and downloadable screen savers and wallpapers; visitors can also watch the trailer as well as a brief clip from the film.

anorexia nervosa—eating disorder in which the victim, usually a teenage girl or young woman, has a distorted view of her own body in which she regards herself as obese; to lose weight, an anorexia victim refuses to eat.

bulimia—eating disorder in which the victim, usually a teenage girl or young woman, eats a great deal then tries to shed weight by purging, often by inducing herself to vomit.

champagne—a sparkling wine, originally named for a region of France noted for producing the beverage.

draft—in wartime, power executed by a government to call up citizens for military service.

ensemble—in the theater or films, a production performed by a large cast with no specific lead actor or actress.

fraud—theft committed by trickery or deceit.

gig—job for professional musicians.

lyrics—words to a song.

mentor—an older and wiser person who helps guide a young person.

pilot—television show produced on an experimental basis to determine whether there is sufficient audience interest to develop a full series.

primary—election staged to select candidates to represent their political parties in the general election.

producers—movie executives who provide financing and arrange other business details involved in developing the film.

psychologist—a doctor who studies human behavior and the workings of the mind.

publicist—professional hired to represent a celebrity, executive, government official or other individuals in contacts with news reporters.

serial killer—murderer whose victims are usually chosen at random yet often fit into a pattern that has meaning to the killer.

suicidal—inclination to take one's own life, usually driven by mental illness.

take—in movies, a scene that is filmed; often, the director requests many takes of the same scene until he or she is satisfied with the result.

tutor—private teacher hired to educate a single student.

zoologist—scientist who studies the lives and habits of animals.

ABOUT THE AUTHOR

Hal Marcovitz lives in Chalfont, Pennsylvania, with his wife Gail and daughters Ashley and Michelle. He is the author of nearly 100 books for young readers, including *LeBron James*, which is also in the POP CULTURE: A VIEW FROM THE PAPARAZZI series.

Picture Credits

page

2: Feature Photo Service
6: Paramount Pictures/NMI
9: WireImage Entertainment
10: New Millennium Images
12: Dooney & Bourke/NMI
15: UPI Photo/Laura Cavanaugh
17: Walt Disney Pictures/KRT
20: Big Pictures USA
22: PFS/NMI
25: Buena Vista Pictures/NMI
26: InterFoto USA/Sipa
28: Splash News
31: Ace Pictures

32: Splash News
34: Casablanca/PRN Photos
37: 20th Century Fox Pictures/NMI
39: Ace Pictures
40: Picturehouse/NMI
42: New Millennium Images
43: New Millennium Images
44: WENN Photo
46: Splash News
49: New Millennium Images
51: The Weinstein Company/MGM
53: FilmMagic
54: UPI Photo/Jim Ruymen

Front cover: Fashion Wire Daily
Back cover: 20th Century Fox Pictures/NMI